🍒 BOOK REVIEW

Fans of the Polk Street School will be happy to have another installment, and new fans will be made.

from SCHOOL LIBRARY JOURNAL

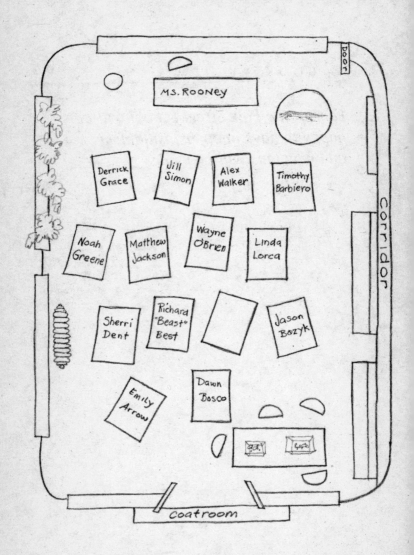

Weekly Reader Books presents

THE BEAST
WHO WAS AFRAID

Original Title: Purple Climbing Days

Patricia Reilly Giff

Illustrated by Blanche Sims

DELACORTE PRESS/NEW YORK

Delacorte Press
1 Dag Hammarskjold Plaza
New York, N.Y. 10017

This work was first published as a Dell Yearling Book.

Manufactured in the United States of America

Library of Congress Cataloging in Publication Data

Giff, Patricia Reilly.
Purple climbing days.

(The Kids of the Polk Street School; no. 9)
Summary: With the help of the meanest substitute
teacher in the whole school Richard "Beast" Best
learns a lesson about fear.
[1. Fear—Fiction. 2. Schools—Fiction]
I. Sims, Blanche, ill. II. Title.
III. Series: Kids of the Polk Street
School; no. 9.
PZ7.G3626Pu 1986   [E]
ISBN 0-385-29500-6
Library of Congress Catalog Card Number: 85-32542

To Helene Steinhauer

THE BEAST
WHO WAS AFRAID

Chapter 1

Richard Best rushed down the hall.

He couldn't wait to get in the classroom.

"Faster," he said to his friend Emily Arrow.

They started to run.

"No running," shouted the sixth-grade monitor.

They slowed down a little.

They turned the corner.

They burst into Room 113.

Today was skink day.

Everyone was in the classroom ahead of them.

All the kids.

Ms. Rooney.

Mrs. Stewart, the student teacher, who used to be Ms. Vincent.

Matthew Jackson poked Richard on the arm. "Hey, Beast," he said. "It's going to be a great day."

Richard nodded. Skink day, he thought.

"Climbing day," said Matthew.

Richard closed his eyes for a second.

Climbing day.

He had forgotten all about it.

He was supposed to climb the rope in gym.

Climb it to the top.

He didn't even like to climb the monkey bars.

"Today I'm going to grab that rope . . ." Matthew began. "Today I'm going right up there."

Richard put his books in his desk.

Today was the day he was going to fall off the gym ceiling. He was going to break his neck.

2

"Look, Beast," Matthew said. He jumped on his chair.

He stretched his arms over his head.

He made believe he was holding the rope.

He raised one foot in the air. "Right to the top. . . ."

Ms. Rooney looked up from her desk. "Matthew Jackson," she said. "It's too early in the morning to start."

Matthew jumped off his chair. "See what I mean?" he told Richard. "That's the way I'm going to climb."

Richard didn't answer.

He thought about the fat brown rope.

The fat brown rope with the fat brown knots.

It was hanging down from the gym ceiling.

He felt dizzy just thinking about it.

He rubbed his hands on his jeans.

Think of the skink, he told himself.

He looked back at the science table.

3

Wayne was supposed to bring in the skink tank. He said he had one at home.

The only tank on the table was the fish tank.

"Hey," Richard said. "Where's the skink tank?"

Matthew raised his shoulders in the air.

"How can we have a skink if we don't have a skink tank?" Richard asked.

"Don't worry," Wayne said from his seat. "It'll be here on time."

"Last call for lunch money," Ms. Rooney said.

Richard poked his head in his desk.

No lunch.

No lunch money either.

He went to the front of the room. "I forgot my—"

"That's no way to start the week," said Ms. Rooney. She reached into her purse. "Pay me back tomorrow."

Richard nodded. "What time is the skink coming?" he asked.

Ms. Rooney put a check next to his name. "Chocolate milk or white?"

"Chocolate," he said. "What time is—"

Ms. Rooney looked up. "This is Monday."

"Right," said Richard.

"You forgot," said Ms. Rooney. "Wednesday is skink day."

Richard went back to his seat.

Monday.

Some kind of chopped-up stuff for lunch.

And no skink.

Matthew was standing next to his desk. He was making circles in the air with his foot. "I'm warming up," he said. "For the climbing."

Richard swallowed.

"Line up," said Ms. Rooney. "Time for gym."

Slowly Richard went to the front of the room.

He wished he could hide somewhere until gym was over.

Chapter 2

The class went down the hall.

At the front of the line Ms. Rooney stopped.

Mrs. Kara was working on a bulletin board.

Pink letters marched along the top.

MOTHER'S DAY IS COMING

"Looks great," said Ms. Rooney.

Mrs. Kara sighed. "Blue Monday," she said. "I need a longer weekend."

Ms. Rooney nodded. "I know what you mean."

Blue Monday, Richard told himself.

It was worse than blue Monday.

It was purple Monday.

Ms. Rooney turned around. "This is a snake line," she said.

The class straightened the line.

Richard tried to keep his head in back of Matthew's ears.

They started to move again.

Richard passed the bulletin board.

Mrs. Kara was putting a row of tulips along the bottom.

They looked like kindergarten flowers.

Baby flowers.

He flicked his finger at one of the stems.

"If you don't mind," Mrs. Kara said.

He ducked his head and kept going.

The class marched into the gym.

Richard looked up.

The ceiling was high.

Almost high enough for an airplane.

He looked down.

He didn't want to see the rope.

"Have a good time," Ms. Rooney said.

She went out to the hall again.

Richard looked around.

He wondered where Mr. Bell, the gym teacher, was.

"Snaggle doodles," yelled Emily. "The rope."

Emily grabbed the rope. "I can do it with my eyes closed," she said. "I can almost do it with one hand."

"Go, Emily," yelled Matthew. "I'm right behind you."

Emily started up the rope.

Richard closed his eyes.

"Hurry," yelled Matthew. "I'm next."

Just then the door opened.

It was Mrs. Miller, the meanest substitute teacher in the school.

9

She was wearing blue shorts and a blue sweatshirt.

She looked like a big blue hippopotamus.

A blue hippopotamus with little skinny legs and black sneakers.

"I can swing like Tarzan," Emily yelled.

Mrs. Miller looked up.

She blew her whistle. "Get down here this minute," she shouted.

Emily started down.

"Who told you to climb?" Mrs. Miller said. "And without a gym teacher here to watch you."

Emily jumped off the rope. "I'm tough," she said. "I won't fall."

"I don't want to hear another word," said Mrs. Miller. She turned to the class. "Today I'm Mr. Bell."

Everyone laughed a little.

Richard raised his hand quickly. "I can't do climbing today."

He crossed his fingers. "My mother said."

Mrs. Miller stared at him.

"I want to climb," he said.

He crossed his fingers in back of him. "I'm dying to climb. Right to the top."

Mrs. Miller was still looking at him.

"My mother said I can't." Richard shook his head. He tried to look sad.

Mrs. Miller frowned. "We're not climbing ropes today," she said. "We're going to play 'A tisket, a tasket, a green and yellow basket.' "

Everybody made a groaning sound.

Richard took a deep breath.

He was saved.

"It was my favorite game when I was young," said Mrs. Miller.

"That's a baby game," Emily said under her breath. "It's for kindergarten kids."

Mrs. Miller blew her whistle. "You're not playing anything," she told Emily. "Sit on the bleachers."

"Too bad we can't climb," Richard told Matthew.

Matthew looked as if he wanted to cry. "I was waiting to climb all weekend," he said.

"It's probably your fault, Beast," said Jason Bazyk. "All that stuff about your mother."

"Maybe Mr. Bell will be back soon," Richard said. "Maybe he just has a cold."

He waved his hand in the air.

"Yes?" Mrs. Miller asked.

"Did Mr. Bell break his leg?" he asked.

Richard tried to cross his toes in his sneakers.

Then he uncrossed them. It wasn't nice to wish Mr. Bell had broken his leg.

"Of course not," Mrs. Miller said.

Richard watched Emily go over to the bleachers.

On the way she grabbed the rope.

She looked back at Mrs. Miller.

Emily had her worst mad face, Richard thought.

13

Emily was much tougher than he was.

Jason came over to him. "This is all your fault," he said. "And your mother's too."

"What's the matter with your mother anyway?" Timothy Barbiero asked.

"Nothing," Richard said.

He thought about his mother.

His mother didn't know they were going to climb.

She probably would have been glad.

She probably would have said, "That's great."

Richard shook his head.

They started to play 'A tisket, a tasket.'

Nobody even called on him.

Chapter 3

It was Wednesday.

Skink day, at last.

Beast and Emily went down the hall.

On the way to their class they passed the gym.

Richard opened the door a tiny bit.

They peeked inside.

Mrs. Miller was in front of the bleachers.

She was jumping up and down on her little skinny legs.

"Snaggle doodles," said Emily. "No climbing again."

She made a face.

Richard tried to make a mad face too.

"I'm going to tell Ms. Rooney," said Emily. "Or even Mr. Mancina. Mr. Bell wants us to climb."

Richard swallowed. "Maybe you'd better not."

"Hey," said Emily. "Here comes Wayne."

Wayne was carrying a big fish tank.

Next to him was Matthew Jackson.

Matthew was carrying his own books under one arm. He had Wayne's under the other.

He was holding two paper bag lunches with his teeth.

Richard could see the tops of the lunch bags were wet from Matthew's mouth.

He wondered if Wayne minded.

They marched into the classroom.

Richard tapped Emily on the shoulder.

He had to tell her not to ask about climbing.

He'd say . . .

What could he say?

Maybe he could say his mother would be mad.

But everyone was rushing back to the science table.

Richard rushed back too.

He grabbed a spot next to the tank.

He stood right next to Emily.

"Listen, Emily," he began. "You'd better not—"

The door opened.

It was Mr. Mancina, the principal. He had a brown box in his hands.

"It's the skink," said Emily. "Finally. We have a class pet."

"We've had fish all along," Wayne said.

"That doesn't count," Emily said. "Everyone has fish. A skink is better."

Everyone crowded around the table.

18

Richard held on to the edge. He didn't want anyone to push him out of the way.

"Don't tell—" he began.

Mr. Mancina came to the back of the room. "Excuse me," he said to Richard.

Richard had to move over.

He tried to squeeze between Timothy and Matthew.

Matthew had wet the bed last night.

Richard held his fingers over his nose. He tried to breathe from his mouth.

At the same time he tried to get Emily's attention.

Matthew looked at Richard.

Richard made believe he was scratching his nose.

Mr. Mancina put the box into the tank.

Then he opened the top of the box.

Everyone leaned over.

"Psst," Richard said to Emily.

"He's down at the bottom of the box," Matthew said. "I can see some brownish—"

"Grayish—" said Jason.

"Here he comes," said Matthew.

"He looks like a dinosaur," said Jill Simon.

"He's a lizard," said Ms. Rooney. "That means he's related to a snake."

"I don't like snakes," said Jill. "That means I might not like a skink."

"He's cold-blooded like a snake," Ms. Rooney said. "His body stays about as warm or cold as the air he's in."

Richard gave Emily a little kick under the table.

"Ouch," Emily said.

"Careful," said Mr. Mancina.

"He's a big one," Wayne said. "Longer than my pencil."

"Maybe he's hungry," said Timothy.

"We could give him some of Drake and Harry's fish food," Emily said.

Mr. Mancina shook his head. "He eats crickets."

"Yuck," Jill said.

"He thinks they're delicious," Mr. Mancina said.

He reached into his pocket.

He pulled out a small white box.

"Here," he told Jill. "Take these."

Jill reached out. "What . . ."

"Skink dinner," said Mr. Mancina. "Crickets."

"Yeow," said Jill.

She backed away from the table.

Mr. Mancina dropped the box.

"You're standing on my foot," Matthew told Jill. "I'm caving in."

The black crickets scattered across the table.

Four people screamed.

Richard opened his mouth. "Emily," he said without making any noise.

Emily scooped up a cricket. "What?"

"The climbing," he said. "Don't—"

"Right," said Emily.

"Look at that guy go," Matthew yelled.

Emily tapped Mr. Mancina on the arm. "How come we can't climb?"

"Climb?"

Richard leaned over the tank. He held his breath. The skink was looking at him.

"In the gym," Emily said. "Mr. Bell is absent. Now Mrs. Miller won't let us climb."

Mr. Mancina started for the door. He winked at them. "Better give a lesson on cricket catching," he told Ms. Rooney.

Then he went out to the hall.

Jill started to cry. "I'm not sitting in here," she said. "Suppose I sit on a cricket?"

"He'll be squished," said Timothy.

"Flatter than a pancake," Jason said.

"Flatter than a potato chip," said Wayne.

"That's enough," Ms. Rooney said.

"Maybe we'll get to climb tomorrow," said Emily.

"Great," Matthew said. He gave Richard a little punch.

"Great," said Richard.

The skink opened its mouth. Its tongue darted back and forth at Richard.

Richard darted his tongue back and forth too.

"He's a brave guy, that skink," said Jason.

"Right," Richard said.

The skink was still looking at him.

Richard wondered if the skink knew he was afraid.

He hoped not.

He stepped back from the tank.

The skink was still staring at him.

Richard sighed.

The skink knew. He was sure of it.

Chapter 4

It was after school.

Richard was alone in the classroom.

He could hear a cricket chirping.

It must have been in someone's desk.

Richard was board monitor for May.

It was a great job.

The greatest.

He sloshed water over the board.

The water ran down in dark lines.

Then he ran along next to the ledge.

He raced the sponge along the ledge too.

He was probably the fastest board monitor in the world.

He looked at the erasers.

They were full of chalk.

He was supposed to take them outside.

He had to clap them near the gym doors.

But Jason and Matthew and Timothy were in the gym. Climbing.

Instead Richard clapped the erasers in the air.

The dust made him cough.

He went over to the skink tank.

Only the skink's head was showing.

The rest of it was buried under the sawdust stuff at the bottom.

The skink looked up at him.

Richard made a friendly face at it.

He tried to look as brave as he could.

"Hey, Rocky," he said.

The skink didn't move.

"Hey, Spiderman."

"What are you doing?" Jim the custodian asked. He was standing at the door.

"Trying to find a skink name," Beast said. "A brave one. What do you think of Mr. T?"

Jim sprinkled green sawdust on the floor. "Sounds all right to me."

Beast stared at the skink.

The skink was staring back.

"I'm not sure he likes it," Beast said.

"Listen," Jim said. "How about taking the erasers outside? Clean them up a little."

"You don't think they look clean?" Beast asked.

Jim began to sweep. "They look like a mess."

"Well," said Beast. He tapped on the tank. "I think it's getting late."

"Aren't you Ms. Rooney's board monitor?" Jim asked.

Richard nodded a little.

"Got to do your best," Jim said.

Richard sighed. "I guess so."

He picked up the erasers.

Slowly he went downstairs.

He clapped an eraser on the stairway wall.

It left a square white mark.

He made two more marks.

They looked like an *F*.

F for ferocious. Ferocious Freddie the skink.

"Young man," a voice said.

It was Mrs. Kettle, the sixth-grade teacher.

She was a tough one.

Almost as tough as Mrs. Miller.

"Did you make those chalk marks?"

Richard rubbed at them with his sleeve.

Mrs. Kettle came down the stairs.

"When I come up again," she said, "these marks had better be gone."

She turned the corner.

Richard spit on his fingers.

He rubbed the wall a little.

27

Then he stood back.

Not bad.

He raced down the stairs.

He looked in the gym window.

Matthew was climbing up the rope.

He ducked past.

He opened the back door and went outside.

He clapped the two erasers thirty-three times.

There was dust all over the place.

Then he went back inside.

Jason was standing at the door. "Hey, Beast," he said. "Come on in here."

Beast shook his head. "Can't."

"Matthew's almost to the top," Jason said. "He's climbing like a monkey."

Richard waved the erasers around. "Jim's waiting for these."

"Just take a quick look," Jason said.

Richard took a step into the gym.

Matthew was hanging on the rope.

He was halfway to the ceiling.

The rope was swinging back and forth.

Richard closed his eyes.

"What's the matter?" Jason asked.

Matthew started to shimmy down.

Richard opened his eyes. "Nothing."

"You're not afraid?" Jason asked.

"Nuh uh," Richard said. "Not a bit."

"How come your mother said you can't climb the rope?"

"Uh . . ." Richard began.

"You're afraid," said Jason.

"Am not," Richard said.

Matthew jumped down the last foot.

He came over to them. "Great stuff," he said. "Excellent."

"Give it a try," Jason told Richard.

Richard shook his head. "My mother said . . ." He tried to think. "My mother said I have a trick knee."

"What's that?" Matthew said.

Richard tried to remember. He had heard his mother say that his Uncle Pete had one.

"I never heard of a trick knee," said Jason.

"We all have it in my family," Richard said. "My Uncle Pete. My father. Holly. . . ."

"Wow," Matthew said. "What's it look like?"

"Well," Richard began. "When you climb it blows up, sort of. It's dangerous."

Just then Mrs. Kettle stuck her head in the door.

"What are you doing in here? Climbing ropes? Without a teacher?" Mrs. Kettle shook her head. "Dangerous. Very dangerous. Out of the gym. This minute."

Then she looked at Richard. "Did you clean those marks?"

"Yes," Richard said. He edged toward the door.

Mrs. Kettle went down the hall.

"I'm not afraid of danger," Richard said. "But I promised my mother."

He hurried out the back door.

Halfway home he saw he was still carrying the erasers.

Then he remembered. His sister, Holly, was waiting in front of school for him.

He hoped Jason and Matthew didn't ask her about her trick knee.

Chapter 5

It was a rainy day.

Richard walked into the kitchen.

"I don't need boots," Richard told his mother.

"He does so," said Holly. "He's always walking in puddles."

"I do not," Richard said. He opened the cabinet door.

"I'll drive you," his mother said. "What are you doing there?"

"I need a potato," he said. "I'm the potato person today."

"You're a potato head," said Holly. "Every day."

"Want a potato in the face?" Richard asked. He raised his arm.

His mother grabbed his wrist. "Why a potato?"

"It's for the skink," Richard said.

He made a face at Holly. "He needs it. We cut it up. Then he can lick it. It's wet."

"What about water?"

"He gets that too. This is extra."

He stuck the potato in his raincoat pocket.

He picked up his books and started for the driveway.

He watched Holly over his shoulder.

She ran to get ahead of him.

She always wanted to sit in the front.

At the last minute he dived for the car.

He beat her there by half a second.

"It's not fair," Holly told his mother. "He always gets to sit in the front."

"Your turn next time," his mother said. She pulled out of the driveway.

Richard watched the rain against the window. "What's a trick knee?" he asked.

His mother raised her shoulders. "Uncle Pete has one. It's nothing much."

"Jason asked me about that yesterday," Holly said.

Richard turned around. "What did you say?"

"I told him to get lost. He's as crazy as you are."

Richard swallowed.

There was only one thing to do.

Climb the rope.

He had to do it.

Right now.

Before everyone else got to school.

He was going to race up that rope.

Right up to the gym ceiling.

Faster than Matthew.

Faster even than Mr. Bell.

Then he wouldn't be afraid anymore.

He tried to swallow. His mouth was dry.

"Do it," he said under his breath.

"Richard's talking to himself," Holly told his mother.

"That's all right," his mother said. "I talk to myself, too, sometimes."

"Really?" Richard said.

"Really," his mother said. She pulled up in front of school.

Richard opened the car door. He dashed up the path.

He made sure to jump over the puddles.

Then he turned to wave at his mother.

He went straight to the gym.

No one else was there yet.

He dropped his yellow raincoat on the floor.

He put his books on top of it.

Then he went over to the rope.

It had a bunch of fat knots. They went all the way to the top.

"Just grab the first knot," he said aloud.

His voice sounded strange in the empty gym.

He jumped up a little and held on.

The rope began to sway.

He held on tight.

"Nothing to it," he said. He touched the floor with one foot.

The rope stopped moving.

Now the next knot.

He'd really have to get off the floor.

He looked up.

He put one hand up a little higher.

He took his foot off the floor.

The rope started to wiggle.

"Don't pay attention," he said.

He tried to move the other hand.

Suppose he got up high?

37

Suppose he fell?

Fell on his head?

Broke his leg?

Broke his arm?

Had to get stitches like Drake Evans did last year?

No good.

He put his feet on the floor again.

Just then the door opened.

It was Jason and Timothy Barbiero.

"What are you doing in here?" Jason said.

"I was climbing the rope," said Richard.

"You didn't get very far," Timothy said.

"No," Richard said.

"I thought you had a trick knee or something," Jason said.

"It's all better," Richard said.

"Then climb the rope," said Jason.

"Can't right now," Richard said.

He walked across the gym.

He picked up his books and his raincoat.

"Scared," he heard Jason whisper.

Richard banged out the gym door. He went down the hall to his classroom.

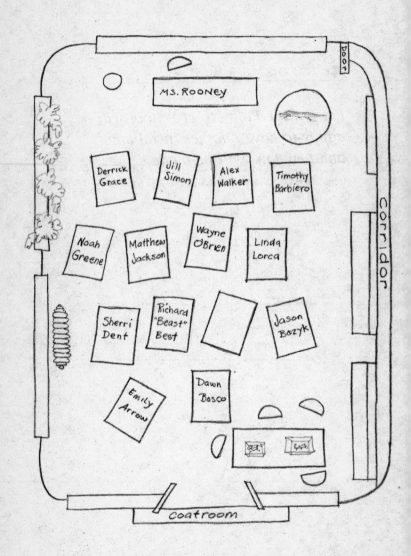

Chapter 4

It was after school.

Richard was alone in the classroom.

He could hear a cricket chirping.

It must have been in someone's desk.

Richard was board monitor for May.

It was a great job.

The greatest.

He sloshed water over the board.

The water ran down in dark lines.

Then he ran along next to the ledge.